DO YOU PROMISE NOT TO BUY A TICKET?

Written by Tracey Özdemir

Illustrated by Joshua Allen

AuthorHouse™ UK Ltd.
1663 Liberty Drive
Bloomington, IN 47403 USA
www.authorhouse.co.uk
Phone: 0800.197.4150

Published by AuthorHouse: 10/23/2015

ISBN: 978-1-5049-8970-1 (sc)
ISBN: 978-1-5049-8971-8 (e)

Print information available on the last page.

Any people depicted in stock imagery provided by Thinkstock are models,
and such images are being used for illustrative purposes only.
Certain stock imagery © Thinkstock.

This book is printed on acid-free paper.

Because of the dynamic nature of the Internet, any web addresses or links contained in this book may have changed
since publication and may no longer be valid. The views expressed in this work are solely those of the author and do not
necessarily reflect the views of the publisher, and the publisher hereby disclaims any responsibility for them.

authorHOUSE®

To all who give love and hope.

But most of all, this book is dedicated to Daisy Shepherdson. The little girl who made a splash into my life like a playful dolphin. With her blonde, curly hair and her cheeky smile and her pure love of all animals, she and the plea of the dolphins were my inspiration for this book.

Also to my daughter, Abbie-Jo, a dolphin defender who has so much love and generosity in her heart. A daughter to be proud of, but most of all, a daughter who I can call my best friend.

This book would never have been possible without wonderful, compassionate friends who have worked so hard to raise the funds to make this book happen. There are too many to mention individually, but you all know who you are. Robert Urquhart and Karen Flynn, it has been a long journey, but we have made it to the end. And my dear friend Trenda Meacham, a true whale warrior, your strength and encouragement has kept me going. I thank you all for having faith in me. Without each and every one of you, this book would not have been possible. I also dedicate this book to every dolphin/whale defender; together we are the voice of the voiceless.

And to our finned friends; to all those that were taken in Taiji. I am sorry. I will never forget you. Until the last tank is empty, we will always fight for you. They say where there is love there is hope. I say where there is captivity there is always freedom.

Tracey Özdemir, Dolphin Lady

One very rainy afternoon, Daisy Dot and Pippi were watching a television show about dolphins. Pippi's eyes were wide, and she wagged her tail.

'Wow!' said Daisy Dot. 'Look at them jump through hoops. They really are very clever. They do all kinds of tricks.' She looked at Pippi with excitement. 'Tomorrow we're going to the dolphin park to see the dolphins.'

Pippi wagged her tail even faster.

The next day, Daisy Dot and Pippi took the bus to the dolphin park. They were very excited indeed and wondered what tricks the dolphins would perform. They hopped off the bus and went straight to the entrance to buy their tickets. They could not wait to see the dolphin show.

When they went inside, they saw a tank full of water that looked like a swimming pool. Daisy Dot thought it seemed very small. The audience sat in seats all around the tank to watch the show. Daisy Dot and Pippi found empty seats and sat down and waited for the show to begin.

Oh my! When the show began, the noise of the music and the audience's clapping and cheering was so loud that it hurt Pippi's ears. The dolphins performed all kinds of tricks, and each time one of them finished, the dolphin trainer blew her whistle and gave the dolphin a fish.

When the show was over and everyone started to leave, Daisy Dot and Pippi went over to the small tank to take a closer look at the dolphins. One of the dolphins, Jonas, was just floating near the surface of the water.

Daisy Dot said to Pippi, 'He looks very sad.'

Jonas heard Daisy Dot say this. He swam over to them and said, 'I am very sad.'

'Oh, but why?' asked Daisy Dot.

Jonas started to cry, and he told Daisy Dot and Pippi, 'You see, this tank is not my home.'

'But where is your home?' asked Daisy Dot.

'My home is in the ocean with my family,' said Jonas.

'How did you get here?' asked Daisy Dot.

'One day I was swimming with my pod.'

'What is a pod?' asked Daisy Dot.

'A pod is a family,' replied Jonas. 'It was winter, and we were swimming to warmer waters. As we swam past a place called Taiji in Japan, all of a sudden boats making a lot of noise came towards us.

'As the boats got closer, we could *see* men on them with long metal poles that they dragged in the water. At their ends of the poles, the men banged on the poles with hammers. We called them "banger boats". The very, very loud noise echoed horribly underwater. We were all frightened and got very confused, and we lost our way. We just wanted to swim away from the boats that were making the noise, but the boats seemed to surround us.

'So we just kept swimming forward. We swam so fast and sometimes dived so deep that we became tired. We tried to stay together. We finally came to a little cove in Taiji, but the men on the boats dropped nets behind us so we could not escape. We were so frightened. I stayed close to my mother.

'Then divers jumped into the water. Everyone in my pod panicked, and we splashed hard with our fluke tails. Some of us got caught in the nets. One diver clung to my mother, and then he tied rope around her fluke tail and dragged her to shallow waters. She and many others from my pod were taken this way. We could not see them in the shallows, as they were taken behind plastic covers.

'The noise from behind the covers was awful. My mother and other family members splashed and screamed. I knew the men were hurting them. Then the water turned red, and everything was silent. I knew then that my mother and most of my family were dead.

'The rest of us feared for our lives, but when the men came for us, I heard one man say, "These ones look beautiful, and they are good jumpers. These are too good to make into meat. We can sell these for lots of money." They grabbed our tails and pulled us into big slings that lifted us onto small boats called skiffs. The men then took us to very tiny sea pens in a nearby harbour.

'We were sad and terrified. Trainers came every day. They taught us to do tricks. If we did not do the tricks, we did not get any food, but when we did get the food, we got only frozen fish. I do not like frozen fish. My pod had always hunted for fresh fish before this.'

Daisy Dot and Pippi felt sad as they listened.

Jonas continued, 'One day, a man dressed in a suit and carrying a bag came to our pen. He watched us do our tricks. He looked at me and smiled and then looked at the trainer and said, "I will take this one." He then put his hand in the bag, pulled out lots of money, and gave it to the trainer. Then once again the divers came. They put me in a sling and put me in another skiff.

'This time they took me to land. Many people stood near a crate with a small amount of water in it and a big crane. They hooked the sling I was in onto the crane and lifted me into the air. I was so frightened; my heart was beating so fast. I was then lowered into the small crate of water. There was no room to move. Then the crate was lifted onto the back of a big truck. It was very dark. The driver climbed in and started the engine, and we set off down the road. We were on the road for a long time.

'When the journey ended, I heard a lot of noise from planes. We were at an airport. Another crane loaded my small crate onto a plane. Then, not long after, we flew up into the sky. I was tired and scared.

'When we landed, I was then loaded onto another truck. Oh my, was I tired and hungry! The journey from Taiji took days. When the truck finally arrived here, I was told that this would be my new home.'

'But you *seem* happy here,' said Daisy Dot. 'And when you did your tricks, you looked like you were full of joy and smiling.'

Jonas replied, 'People always think we are happy *because* we look like we are smiling, but that is just the natural shape of a dolphin's mouth. If you look into my eyes, you will *see* nothing but sadness.'

Daisy Dot asked Jonas what he did when the audience went home.

Jonas replied, 'I get lonely and bored. This tank is so small that I can only swim in little circles. When I was in the ocean, my pod and I could swim for miles and miles every day in straight lines.' Jonas paused. 'I am so sad here. The trainers give me medicine to stop me from being sad, but it does not work. And I am very hungry. I don't get much food. I get more if I do my tricks, but it is not very nice, as it is not fresh.'

This made Daisy Dot and Pippi even more sad.

Daisy Dot looked into the dolphin's eyes and asked, 'What can Pippi and I do to help you?'

Jonas said, 'That is easy. Tell your friends not to buy a ticket to this show. The money from ticket sales goes to the men on the boats who hunt for dolphins. Tell your friends my story. Tell them that dolphins live in the ocean – and that is the only place where we belong. Tell them to tell their friends. Remember everything I have told you. Please, remember that dolphins like me do not belong in tanks. Some tanks are like swimming pools. They have chlorine in the water, and that makes our skin very sore. The ocean is salt water, and that is where we belong and should live. Please, do not buy a ticket!'

Daisy Dot and Pippi had to say a very sad goodbye. Daisy Dot looked at Jonas and said, 'One day you will be free. I will tell everyone your story. Pippi and I will never forget you, and we promise that we will never again buy a ticket to a dolphin show.'

Daisy Dot and Pippi went home. They never forgot the sad dolphin Jonas, and they never went to another dolphin park. They never *broke* their promise.

At home, Daisy Dot looked at Pippi and *stroked* her shiny coat. She said, 'If only everyone would make the same promise, then every dolphin would be free.'

Do you promise not to buy a ticket?

Daisy Dot's True Facts

1. Dolphins are mammals. This means that mothers nurse their babies with milk.

2. Dolphins can stay underwater up to fifteen minutes, but they cannot breathe underwater.

3. When a dolphin sleeps, only half of the brain sleeps. The other half stays awake so the dolphin can continue to get air to breathe.

4. The largest member of the dolphin family is the orca, also known as the killer whale.

5. Dolphins communicate with each other using whistles and clicking sounds.

6. Dolphins cannot chew their food, as their faces do not have the muscles to chew. Instead, they swallow their food whole

7. Dolphins can swim twenty-five miles per hour

8. Dolphins use echolocation to navigate and find food. Echolocation is determining location with the echoes of high pitch sounds.

9. Dolphins are intelligent.

10. The greatest danger to a dolphin is humans

I have *been* an animal rights activist, especially for dolphins and whales, since I was seven years old. It all started when I was a little girl, and I was taken to a marine park to *see* a captive-dolphin show. Even at this early age I sensed things were wrong, and I started to ask questions that very day. Why was the dolphin in a swimming pool full of chemicals? Why was the dolphin fed frozen fish? Why did the dolphin's eyes look so sad? As the years went *by*, I learned more and more about dolphin and whale captivity. I realized that dolphin therapy is nothing but a scam. Children visiting an animal rescue center, such as a dog shelter, would receive the same benefits from stroking a puppy as they would swimming with a dolphin. Dolphin therapy creates a happy feeling, not a cure. That happy feeling can *be* gained *by* seeing or feeling any cute animal. When I advise parents of the dangers of dolphin and whale captivity, they say "But my child will never *see* a dolphin if these parks did not exist. How will they learn about them?" My answer to that is, "Your child will never *see* a dinosaur, but they still learn all about them."

Then one day while watching TV, Ric O'Barry, the former trainer of Flipper (A 60's TV show about a dolphin), was on a chat show. He is now an activist fighting against captivity. But the part that *shocked* me most was the footage shown of the *barbaric* slaughter of thousands of dolphins that takes place annually from the first day of September all the way through til March in Taiji, Japan. I knew there and then I had to do more. Most people are not aware of how captivity and slaughter go hand in hand or how each captive suffers. I am proud to say I have stood *by* Ric's side at protests for the release and against the slaughter of these incredible beings that have so much intelligence and sensitivity – much more than any human.

My home *seems* to be a favorite place to visit due to my four legged family. My fur family includes two Great Danes and two Yorkshire Terriers. Pippi is one of my little Yorkies, and is often the favorite among young children. Most children in my life love animals and know what I do for the dolphins, and are fully aware of the atrocities and yet this has not given any cause for nightmares and neither have they *been* affected in any physical or mental way.

I find that these children show true compassion through their innocence and love of animals. My friend Vicki Kiely took several young children to the Killing cove in Taiji through The Dolphin Project. These youngsters made amazing mini cove monitors. Their compassion shined from within, even after witnessing a red cove day, which is a day dolphins are hunted and driven into the cove for slaughter. Many of us know it is most children's dream to swim with a dolphin – but what if children were to know the truth about dolphins in captivity? Through this came my idea for a much-needed children's awareness book. I decided to write about how our finned friends are in trouble. Children will learn the facts from a captive dolphin named Jonas. Through this story, children can learn that visiting a marine park only adds to the problem. And they will learn how captivity goes hand in hand with slaughter.

Daisy Dot and Pippi meet a captive dolphin named Jonas, and they learn of dolphins' dreadful experience through Jonas's eyes. After learning of the hard journey that Jonas and his pod have gone through, they are educated about the simplest way to end the captive/slaughter industry.

My hope is that through my *book*, many children will *become* aware and that they will share that awareness with their friends too.

Our orca friends are in great danger too. Daisy Dot and Pippi meet two orcas with a sad tale to tell.

Follow them in the next book, "Be a Voice", and meet Topsy and Dipper to learn of their extraordinary tale.

For more information on how you can help our finned friends:

Please go to the Ric O'Barry's Dolphin Project website

www.DolphinProject.net

For further information on how to adopt a dolphin or orca through the WDC

http://uk.whales.org/

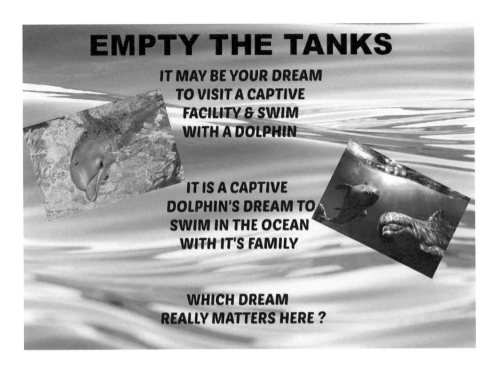

A dolphins dream

Ric O'Barry, Tracey Özdemir (Dolphin Lady) at demonstration
against dolphinaria in Europe. Brussels 2014

The real Pippi

Grade 9 students from Marmaris Campus of Izmir Turk College,
Empty The Tanks Protest Marmaris 2015

Empty The Tanks Demonstration 2015

A very sad captive

The Mini Cove Monitors meet the captives held at Taiji Whale Musem

Vicki Kiely (Dolphin Project), Mini cove monitors (From Gecko School Phuket) at Taiji cove

Sea Pens at Taiji

Trainers with Captives at Taiji

Painted rocks at the edge of the killing cove. To remember every dolphin that was taken.

Photographs by Tracy Harper. .

Photo by Debbie Wilkinson Photography

Lightning Source UK Ltd.
Milton Keynes UK
UKIC03n2307051115
262189UK00008B/38